Studio Fun International
An imprint of Printers Row Publishing Group
A division of Readerlink Distribution Services, LLC
10350 Barnes Canyon Road, Suite 100, San Diego, CA 92121
www.studiofun.com

Printers Row Publishing Group is a division of Readerlink Distribution Services, LLC.
Studio Fun International is a registered trademark of Readerlink Distribution Services, LLC.

All notations of errors or omissions should be addressed to Studio Fun International, Editorial Department, at the above address.

ISBN: 978-0-7944-4373-3
Manufactured, printed, and assembled in Shenzhen, China.
First printing, January 2019. RRD/01/19
23 22 21 20 19   1 2 3 4 5

Disney

Pinocchio

studio fun
INTERNATIONAL

Once upon a time, in a quaint little village, a beautiful wishing star shone brightly in the evening sky. A cricket named Jiminy wandered along the village streets. He saw a lighted window and went inside.

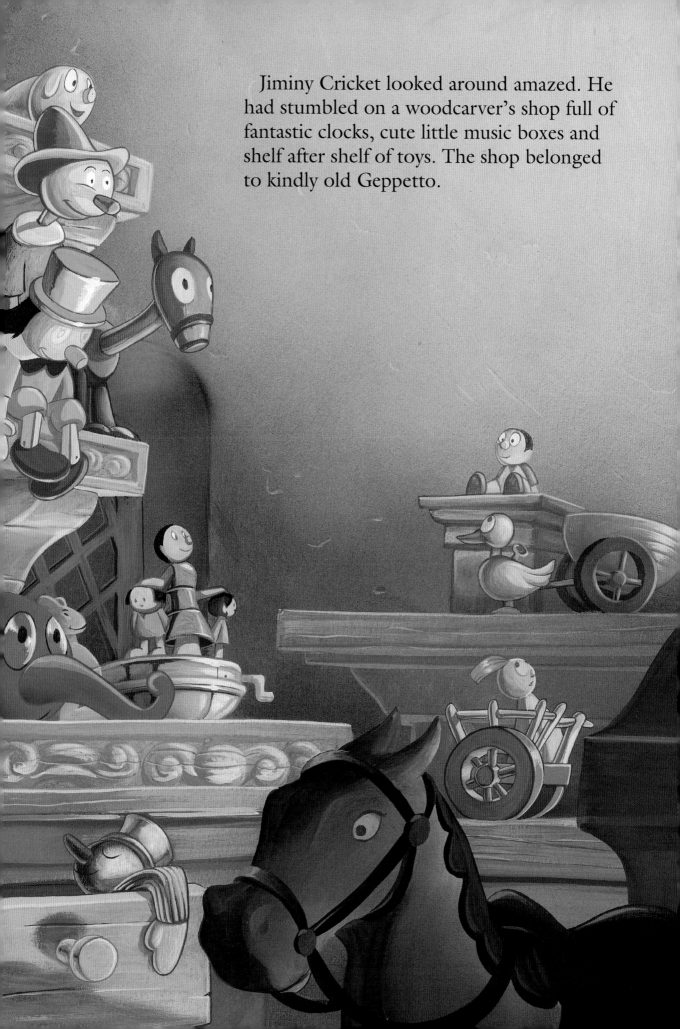

Jiminy Cricket looked around amazed. He had stumbled on a woodcarver's shop full of fantastic clocks, cute little music boxes and shelf after shelf of toys. The shop belonged to kindly old Geppetto.

Geppetto was working on a wooden puppet. He took his paintbrush and carefully painted on eyebrows and a mouth. His cat Figaro and his goldfish Cleo watched as he worked.

"I have just the name for you," Geppetto said when he finished. "Pinocchio!"

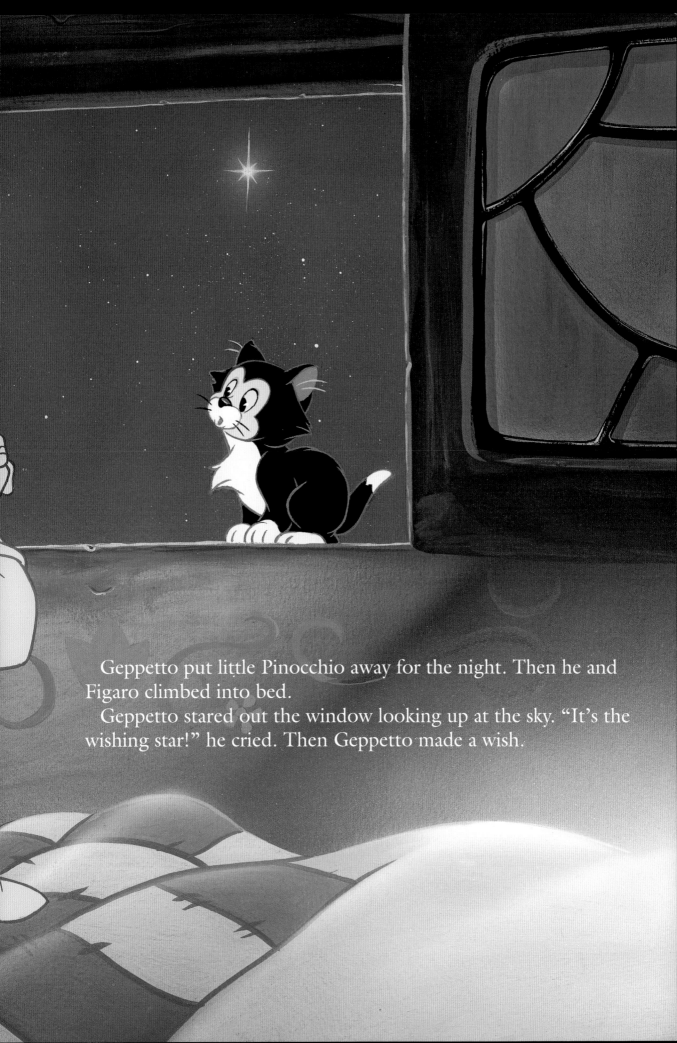

Geppetto put little Pinocchio away for the night. Then he and Figaro climbed into bed.

Geppetto stared out the window looking up at the sky. "It's the wishing star!" he cried. Then Geppetto made a wish.

As Geppetto slept, he dreamed about his wish. He had wished that Pinocchio might be a real boy.

Suddenly, a brilliant light filled Geppetto's room. It sparkled and grew into the beautiful Blue Fairy.

"Good Geppetto," the fairy said, "you deserve to have your wish come true!"

She waved her magic wand over Pinocchio, saying, "Little puppet made of pine, wake! The gift is thine!"

Suddenly, Pinocchio lifted his arms and spoke. "Am I a real boy?" he asked.

"No," the fairy explained. "First you must prove yourself brave, truthful, and unselfish. You must learn to choose between right and wrong."

The Blue Fairy told Pinocchio that he must let his conscience be his guide. And, with a little coaxing from the Blue Fairy, Jiminy Cricket agreed to be his conscience. Then she was gone!

Geppetto, hearing strange noises, jumped out of bed. When he got to his workshop, he saw his little puppet dancing around and singing. Geppetto lifted Pinocchio into the air and hugged him close.

The next morning, Geppetto walked Pinocchio outside and pointed to all the children passing by. "They are going to school," he explained. "Now that you are a little boy, you must go to school, too."

THE GREAT
STROMBOLI
MARIONETTE SHOW

Hoping to make Geppetto proud, Pinocchio hurried off. He didn't realize that two sneaky-looking characters were watching him.

"A live puppet, with no strings!" the fox exclaimed. "We can sell him to Stromboli the puppeteer."

The fox tripped Pinocchio with his cane. "I am J. Worthington Foulfellow, but my friends call me Honest John," he explained. "And this is Gideon," he added, pointing to the cat standing by his side.

Pinocchio looked up at Honest John. "I have to get to school," he explained.

Honest John convinced Pinocchio that school was a waste of time. "Come with us," he coaxed. "We'll make you a star."

Back at Geppetto's workshop, Jiminy Cricket hurried into his coat and hat and ran out the door. He saw Honest John, Gideon, and Pinocchio heading down the street—in the wrong direction.

Soon Jiminy Cricket caught up with Pinocchio and tried
to change his mind. But it was too late. Honest John had
convinced Pinocchio to go on stage. They were going to see
Stromboli the puppeteer.

Honest John led Pinocchio right into Stromboli's greedy hands.

That night, Pinocchio made his stage debut with Jiminy Cricket in the audience. Everyone was amazed to see a singing, dancing puppet with no strings.

When the show was over, the crowd applauded wildly and threw gold coins at Pinocchio's feet.

Pinocchio loved all the attention. And Stromboli loved all the money the little puppet had made him!

Later that night, Pinocchio couldn't wait to get home and tell Geppetto all about his new career. When Stromboli heard Pinocchio talking about going home, he threw him in a cage and locked the door.

As Pinocchio cried and called out for Jiminy, the cricket sneaked into Stromboli's wagon. Jiminy couldn't believe his eyes when he saw Pinocchio locked in a cage.

Meanwhile, poor Geppetto was very worried about his little son. He went out to search for Pinocchio.

Back at Stromboli's wagon, as Jiminy was trying to free Pinocchio, the Blue Fairy appeared. When she asked Pinocchio why he hadn't gone to school, Pinocchio told so many lies that his nose grew.

Pinocchio promised that he would never lie again. The Blue Fairy agreed to give him another chance, freeing him with her wand. Then she disappeared once more.

Jiminy and Pinocchio jumped down from the cage and ran home as fast as they could.

In a nearby tavern, Honest John and Gideon were meeting with the Coachman who liked to lure boys to Pleasure Island. The Coachman promised Honest John and Gideon money if they would help him find some boys.

Soon Honest John and Gideon were back on the streets, where they spotted Pinocchio. Pretending that Pinocchio looked sickly, Honest John convinced the little puppet that he needed some rest and relaxation—on Pleasure Island.

Honest John and Gideon led Pinocchio down the street. They told him all about the wonders of Pleasure Island—games, toys, candy, rides—and it was all free!

Poor Jiminy tried to catch up with them.

Outside the village, Honest John turned Pinocchio over to the Coachman. Pinocchio climbed aboard a stagecoach filled with boys. The Coachman cracked his whip and off they went.

When the boys arrived on Pleasure Island, they could hardly believe their eyes! There were no grown-ups around to tell them what to do. The boys could be as naughty as they liked.

Pinocchio soon made friends with a boy named Lampwick.

"If my mother could see me now, she'd have a fit," he explained to Pinocchio, who was about to sample some sugary treats.

While Pinocchio was busy with Lampwick, Jiminy Cricket explored the island. He came upon the Coachman giving orders to his men. "Shut the doors and lock them tight!"

Jiminy knew he had to find Pinocchio right away!

"Pinocchio! Pinocchio!" Jiminy called, looking around the dark and deserted place. "Where is everybody?"

Jiminy saw a light in the pool hall. There he found Pinocchio and Lampwick playing pool.

"You're coming right home with me!" Jiminy cried.

Lampwick laughed. "You're taking orders from a grasshopper?"

Poor Pinocchio was caught between his new friend and his conscience.

On his way out, Jiminy saw the Coachman and his men putting donkeys in crates. "You boys will bring me a nice price." The Coachman smiled.

Jiminy realized that the donkeys were the boys of Pleasure Island!

Jiminy ran back to warn Pinocchio. But it was too late! Lampwick had already changed into a donkey. Poor Pinocchio stared in horror as he sprouted his own set of donkey ears and a tail.

"Quick! We've got to get out of here!" yelled Jiminy.
Pinocchio and Jiminy Cricket raced across the now-deserted
island, leaving the Coachman and donkeys behind. They
climbed up the sea rocks and jumped into the sea.

The pair finally reached the shore and headed for home. But when they arrived, Geppetto was nowhere to be found.

A dove flying overhead dropped a letter for Pinocchio.

The letter said that Geppetto had gone looking for Pinocchio and had been swallowed by a whale named Monstro! Pinocchio and Jiminy headed back to the sea.

At the bottom of the ocean, they began their search for Monstro. Pinocchio and Jiminy asked every fish and sea creature where to find Monstro. But no one would help them. Soon Pinocchio spotted Monstro just as the monster was waking up.

Meanwhile deep inside Monstro's belly, Geppetto
was hoping for a miracle. "There isn't a fish left,"
he explained to poor starving Figaro and Cleo.
"If the monster doesn't wake up soon, I'm afraid
we are done for!"

Suddenly Monstro started to swim. He was ready for lunch. He opened his gigantic jaws and sucked in an entire school of fish—and Pinocchio along with them!

Pinocchio and the fish swam down the whale's throat and into his giant belly. When he got there, Pinocchio found himself in the arms of a very happy Geppetto.

"We must get out of here," Pinocchio said. "But how?"
Then Pinocchio had an idea. He began chopping up furniture.
"We'll start a fire and make lots of smoke," Pinocchio said. "Then
Monstro will wake up and sneeze us out!"

Monstro soon felt the fire in his belly.

Inside, everyone quickly jumped onto a raft that Geppetto had built and paddled toward the whale's throat. When Monstro let out an enormous sneeze, he blew the raft out to sea.

Monstro was furious. Seeing the raft bobbing up ahead, he smashed it into pieces.

Pinocchio, holding on to Geppetto, swam with all his might. He led Monstro into a collision with the rocks.

Pinocchio had made sure that Geppetto got safely to shore. But when Geppetto looked around for his little son, he found him lying face-down in the water. Geppetto picked Pinocchio up and carried him home.

Once inside, Geppetto laid Pinocchio on his bed. Suddenly the Blue Fairy appeared!

She waved her wand over Pinocchio, saying, "You have proven yourself brave, truthful, and unselfish. Now you will become a real boy!"

The lifeless wooden puppet was suddenly transformed into a real little boy. Geppetto wound his music boxes and they all began to dance. What a celebration they had—the woodcarver, his son, the cat, the goldfish, and a wise cricket named Jiminy!